# The Candy Calamity

DOM-A-TRON
THE OLD ISLANDS
Doomsdome
Burrycanter
UTOPIA
Freedom Island
WIGGAMORE WOODS
SUMA SAVANNA
Rushington
Hive Haven
Furenzy park
Toke-A-Toke
Wonder Well
Capitol
Mushroom Village
Deserted Desert
RAKA RAIN FOREST
Mt. Avalerif
Sky Tree
Snapfast Meadow
CAR-A-LAGO COAST
Starlotte City
Gray Landing

# Home of the Brave

*Welcome to Freedom Island, Home of the Brave, where good battles evil and truth prevails. Learn more about the importance of self-control and taking care of your body by completing the BRAVE Challenge at the back of the book.*

**Watch this video for an introduction to the story and BRAVE Universe!**

Saga Two: Iron Chaos

Book 3

**The Candy Calamity**

Saga Two: Iron Chaos—Book 3

**The Candy Calamity**



Published by BRAVE BOOKS
www.BRAVEbooks.com

ISBN: 978-1-955550-25-3 (paperback)

First edition published in the USA in 2022 by BRAVE BOOKS

Printed in the USA

# The Candy Calamity

**BRAVE BOOKS** and **ZUBY**

Art by **Ali Elzeiny**

BRAVE BOOKS

The Deserted Desert was a hot, empty place;
A hideout for pirates, this wide open space.
A gorilla named Bongo walked, holding his tummy,
Aching and longing for anything yummy.

On the edge of the desert in a small, cozy spot
Lived a caravan of camels who enjoyed being hot.
One camel, called Cooby, invited Team BRAVE
To come to his house with a smile and a wave.

Cooby welcomed his friends. Bongo strolled to the couch;
He sat and said, "Groovy," pulling snacks from his pouch.
Valor vibed with the music that Cooby had made;
On the obstacle course, Rebel stayed out and played.

Cooby

Carter the camel raced in, yelling, “Dude!
Lester the pirate stole most of our food!”
Bongo slurped and then burped, preparing for war.
“Don’t worry; we’ll help!” as he waddled to the door.

The pirates were in-and-out, fast as a whip,
In Lester's amazing new sand-sailing ship.
They grabbed the camels' food, supplies, and tarps, too!
But when Lester saw Bongo, he sang to his crew:

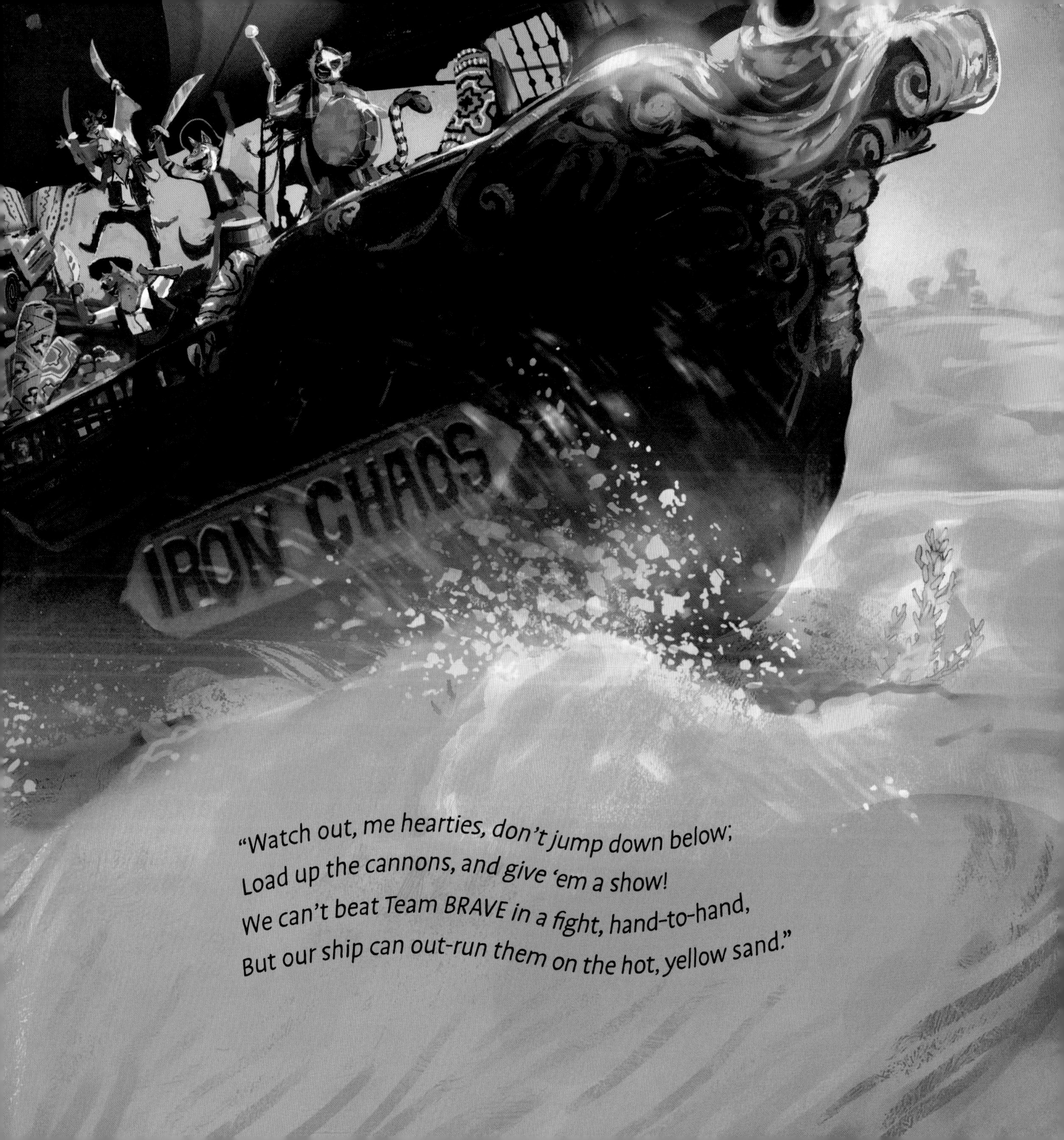


"Watch out, me hearties, don't jump down below;
Load up the cannons, and give 'em a show!
We can't beat Team BRAVE in a fight, hand-to-hand,
But our ship can out-run them on the hot, yellow sand."

Valor called out, “Don’t let them escape!”
But Bongo, he realized, was too out of shape.
He grabbed for the ship, then fell to the sand,
And Lester sailed off, across the vast land.

Bongo and Valor returned in defeat.
The gorilla sank down as he ate something sweet.
Valor was tired and his fur was all sandy.
Bongo just sat there, nom-nom-nom, eating his candy.

Cooby

"What did I miss?" Rebel asked with a frown.

Valor said, "Pirates attacked this small town!

Lester stole half the town's food and supplies."
Bongo mumbled through treats, "We did our best, guys."

"No, we've been lazy," Valor said with conviction.
"We cannot win fights with a candy addiction.
They counted on us, and we let them all down.
We must learn to do better to save their sweet town."

"Let's go, couch potatoes," Rebel said with a smirk.
"It will take running and a lot of hard work,
But add motivation, and we'll win the next fight!"
Bongo grunted and pouted but knew they were right.

Week after week, they hit the course every day,
But Bongo kept dreaming of a candy buffet.
Soon, with some help from Cooby's good guiding,
They were bouncing and leaping, swinging and sliding.

Every day, Cooby made them a warm cactus dinner.
The food wasn't sweet, but Bongo's belly got thinner.
Valor and Bongo took breaks for meals every day,
While Rebel stayed out, preferring to play.

Cooby

After some time, Bongo's muscles grew big.
He swung and moved fast, did some zags and some zigs.
He even beat Rebel as they raced through the town,
But when he looked back, she had BLAT! fallen down.

"My strength is all gone," Rebel trembled and panted.
Valor lifted her head. "Don't take food for granted.
You didn't stop playing when we needed to eat.
Without food for fuel, of course you'll be beat."

"Rebel," said Bongo, "Remember our goal:
Not just to run fast, but to have self-control.
Eating nothing will hurt you; overeating will too.
Cooby's fixed us a meal. Let's get some for you."

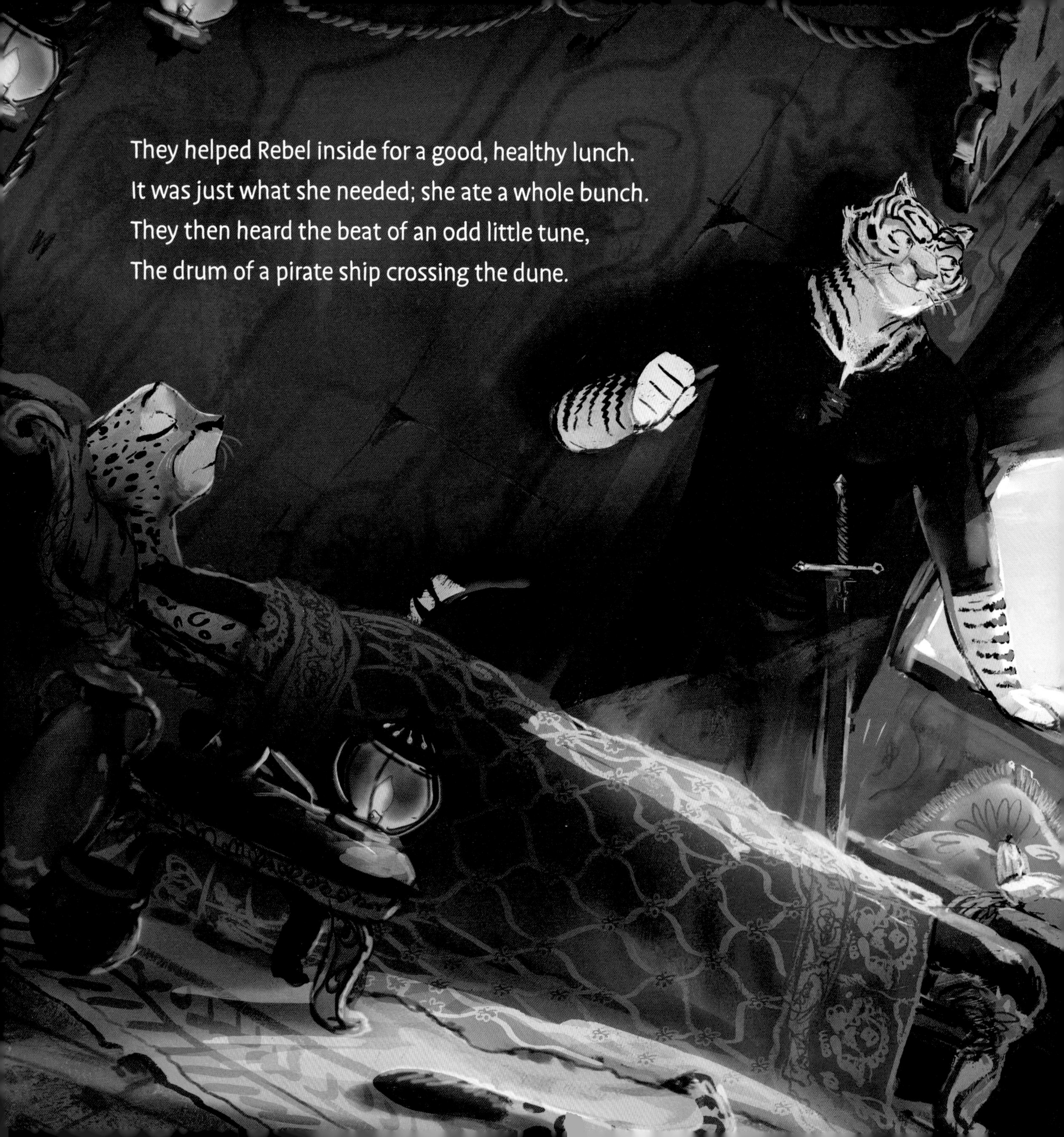

They helped Rebel inside for a good, healthy lunch.
It was just what she needed; she ate a whole bunch.
They then heard the beat of an odd little tune,
The drum of a pirate ship crossing the dune.

Bongo let loose a laugh. “I’m ready this time!
Lester needs a good whoopin’ for his piratey crime.
We’ve got this, Rebel. Take care, and rest here!”
He and Valor dashed out as the huge ship came near.

*We be stealin' supplies for our big master plan.*
*If Team BRAVE cannot stop us, then nobody can!"*

Lester laughed har-har-har, not realizing the fact:
That Team BRAVE wasn't weak; they'd now become jacked!
This time, Bongo and Valor chased the ship with ease.
They caught the ropes and climbed the hull; it was such a breeze.

Once on board the ship, they fought side-by-side
'Til every last pirate had run off to hide.

Valor grabbed the food; the pirates were done.
Lester cowered and squealed, “Ouchy, my drum!”

Defeated, Lester and his pirate crew sailed away.
Because of Team BRAVE, they no longer could stay.
The camels had no reason to fear Lester's gang.
Bongo flexed his muscles as he called out and sang:

*"You pirates are rude, and you started this feud.*
*Why'd you conclude you can steal all our food?*
*If you try to intrude, you'll be barbecued.*
*You don't like our crew? ... Okay dude."*

Cody

They returned all the food once the pirates had fled,
The cactus and fruit, the peanuts and bread.
They thanked Cooby for helping them all reach their goal,
By teaching them a lesson on health and self-control.

They gathered together for a dinner so nice.
Celebrating with dessert, Bongo ate just one slice.
He knew staying healthy was the sweetest of treats.
Tasting victory was better than anything he could eat.

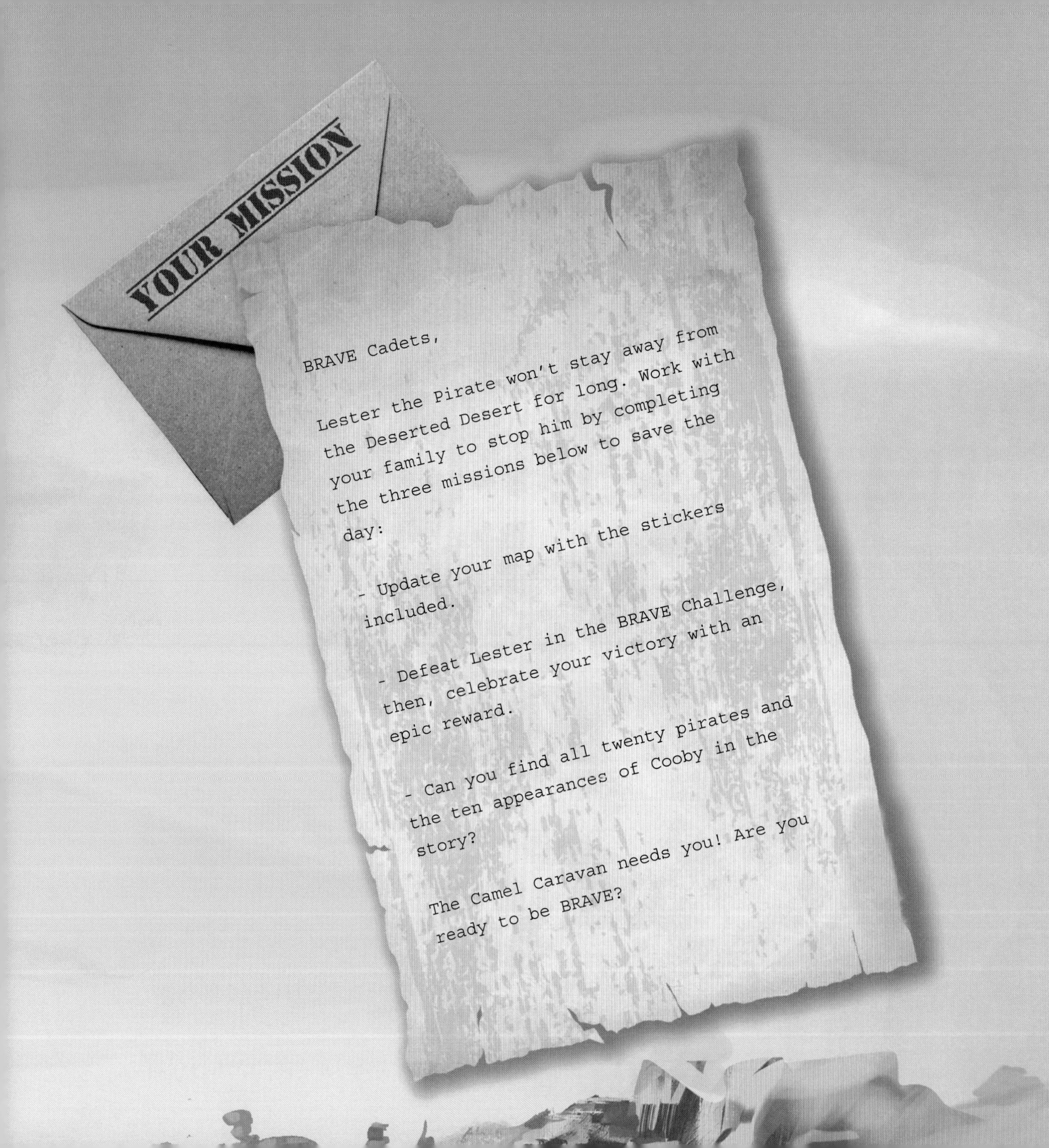


BRAVE Cadets,

Lester the Pirate won't stay away from the Deserted Desert for long. Work with your family to stop him by completing the three missions below to save the day:

- Update your map with the stickers included.

- Defeat Lester in the BRAVE Challenge, then, celebrate your victory with an epic reward.

- Can you find all twenty pirates and the ten appearances of Cooby in the story?

The Camel Caravan needs you! Are you ready to be BRAVE?

# THE BRAVE CHALLENGE

## INTRODUCING... ZUBY

Zuby is an independent rapper, author, podcast host, public speaker, and creative entrepreneur with over one million followers on social media. He was born in England, raised in Saudi Arabia, and is a graduate of Oxford University. He not only has a politically influential voice to the public, but also is a fitness expert and life coach, specifically focusing on mindset, exercise, and nutrition.

### ZUBY SUGGESTS:

"I hope you enjoy this BRAVE Challenge as you pursue a healthier lifestyle for you and your family!"

## INTRODUCTION

Welcome BRAVE Cadets! The BRAVE Challenge is a quick and fun way to drive home key lessons illustrated in the story. In this Brave Challenge, you will be competing against yourself! Push your limits and learn what being disciplined means in your own life.

## ADDITIONAL VIDEO CONTENT

For a fun addition to the BRAVE Challenge experience, scan Iggy Guana's QR code or search for BRAVE Books on YouTube. In the videos linked there, Super Secret Special Agent J explains more about the topic in a way that the whole family will enjoy.

## HOW TO PLAY

To get started, grab a sheet of paper and a pencil so the BRAVE Cadets can keep track of their points. If they can reach a total of 20 points between both games, they win!

Before starting the first game, choose a prize for winning. For example ...

- Making fruit smoothies
- Create an obstacle course in your backyard
- Candle-lit dinner
- Whatever gets your kiddos excited!

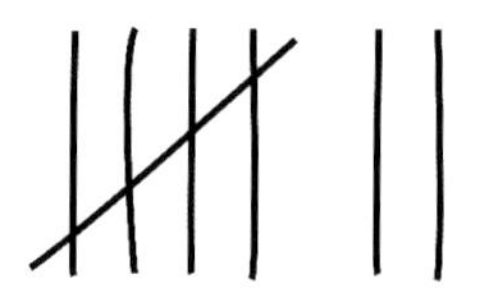


Ready? Let's go!

## GAME #1 - PUSHING THROUGH PUSH-UPS

### OBJECTIVE

Bongo and Rebel are having a hard time being disciplined in keeping up with their exercises. It's your job to help Bongo and Rebel understand the importance of perseverance by pushing past your limits in this challenge.

### LESSON

With the right mindset and goal, you can push past discomfort.

### MATERIALS

A timer for Round 2.

# INSTRUCTIONS

**ROUND 1: PUSH-UPS**

1. Have all the BRAVE Cadets line up on the ground. When you say go, they will start doing as many push-ups as they can.

## BRAVE TIP

Your kids should be pushing themselves, no matter what level they're at. For those who can't manage full push-ups, encourage them to do knee push-ups or sit-ups.

2. ***Secret Step:*** *After the kids say they can't do any more push-ups, tell them that they will earn one point for every additional push-up they can do in the next minute.*

## BRAVE TIP

Don't be afraid to challenge your kids! Only give them points if they are actually pushing past their limits.

**ROUND 2: WALL-SITS**

3. Have all the cadets line up against a wall and hold a wall-sit for as long as they can.
4. ***Secret Step:*** *After the kids say they can't hold the wall-sit any longer, say they'll earn a point for every ten seconds they can keep holding the position.*

## TIME

Brave Cadets will have one minute to do the additional push-ups and wall-sits.

## SCORING

Each cadet earns one point for every additional push-up (max 15 points each) and one point for every 10 seconds of wall-sits (max 6 points each).

Give the whole team the score of the one BRAVE Cadet who did the best each round.

# TALK ABOUT IT

1. In the game, you had to push past your limit to do extra push-ups and wall-sits. When you thought you couldn't do any more, what made you push past the pain?
2. What is something else besides the challenge that you didn't think you would be able to do, but then you pushed yourself and were able to do it? How did you feel after you finished it?

## BRAVE TIP

Parents, tell your kids of a time when you pushed past your limits and what you learned from it.

3. Do you like exercising? What do you like or not like about it?

## ZUBY SUGGESTS

"It's hard for us to enjoy difficult things, but if we push through, we find that hard things are much more rewarding in the end. Take a moment to compare the rewards of working out with the costs."

4. What are some things you do that are exercise?
5. In the story, Bongo had to learn to say no to his desire for candy. What things should you limit in your life in order to be more fit; physically, mentally, or spiritually?

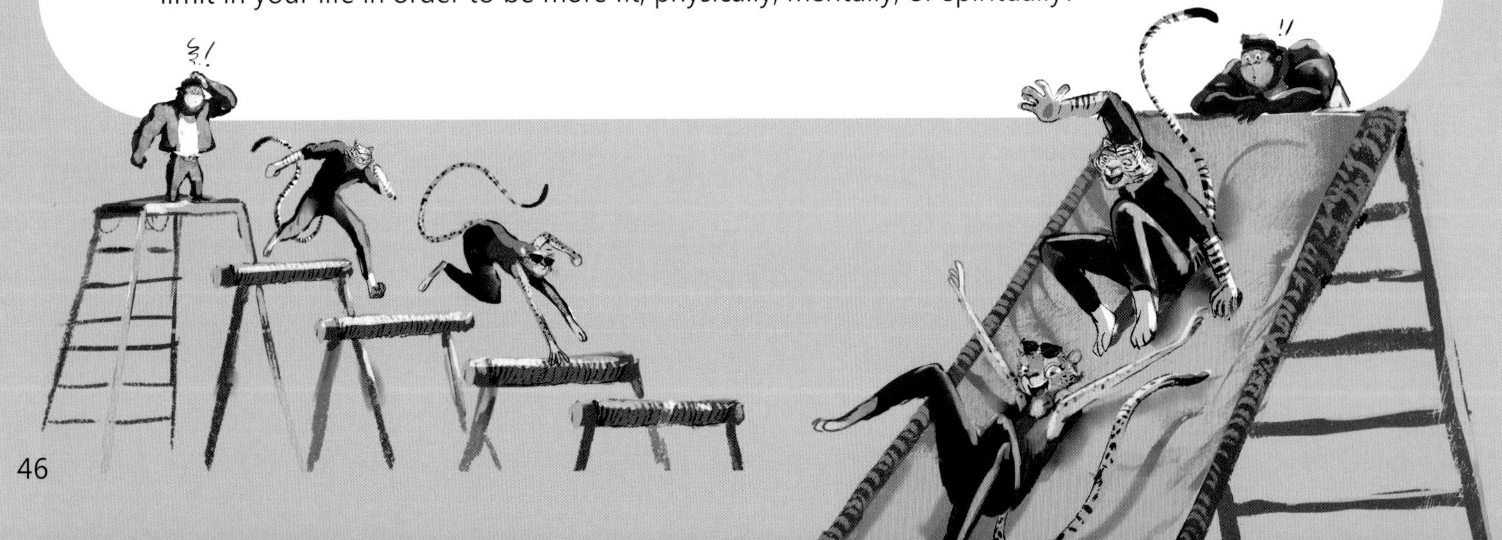

# GAME #2 - STAY THE COURSE

## LESSON

With practice and discipline, you can become stronger.

## OBJECTIVE

BRAVE Cadets! You must prepare for the pirates' attack on the caravan. Race through the obstacle course to get stronger, and see if you can beat your own time!

## MATERIALS

A timer & items for an obstacle course.

# INSTRUCTIONS

1. Parents, help the BRAVE Cadets set up an obstacle course around the house or in your backyard.

### BRAVE TIP

Feel free to make this course as elaborate or as simple as you like to suit your family. Feel free to use any suggestion from the list below. Alternatively, go to a park and choose a path through the playground. Have fun with this!

Suggestions:

- Crawl under a row of chairs.
- Throw a wad of paper into a trashcan.
- Jump between scattered couch cushions.
- Jump between hoola hoops laying on the ground.
- Run around a tree three times.
- Crawl under a string that's tied between objects.

2. Record how long it takes for each BRAVE Cadet to run through the course once.
3. Have the cadets run again, trying to beat their own time.
4. ***Secret Step:*** *Have the cadets run a third time to see if they can improve even more. They will earn one point for every second they improve between this run and the previous one.*

## BRAVE TIP

Parents, take the chance to join in the fun! Don't be shy to run through the obstacle course as well.

### TIMER

Parents will record each BRAVE Cadet's time for each of the three runs.

### SCORING

Identify the cadet who improved their course time the most between the second and third run. Give the whole team one point for each second this cadet cut off his or her time.

# TALK ABOUT IT

1. In the game, you challenged yourself to beat your time with each run. What are some benefits of challenging yourself?
2. Why is it important to keep practicing difficult things?

### ZUBY SUGGESTS

"Exercise is not only about growing physically, but mentally as well. You need practice and discipline because you will always face obstacles in life that will make it harder to achieve your goals."

3. If you were to run this same course five years from now, do you think that your time would be better? Do you think it would be better if you didn't train your body well?
4. In the story, Bongo worked hard to train and eat well so that he was prepared for the pirates' second attack. How can exercising and eating right help you?

### ZUBY SUGGESTS

"A goal is something that you're working towards. Creating goals for yourself can motivate you to work out and make healthier food choices."

5. Too much of a good thing can be damaging. In the story, Rebel focused so much on fitness and exercise that she neglected nutrition and couldn't help the camels. Why do you think it is wise to have a balanced view of exercise and food?

## ZUBY SUGGESTS

"When you live healthily, you equip yourself to help people around you. Rather than exercising to get attention or approval, we should improve ourselves so that we can better care for and focus on other people."

"So, whether you eat or drink, or whatever you do, do all to the glory of God."

**1 Corinthians 10:31** (ESV)

# TALLY ALL THE POINTS TO SEE IF YOU WON!

## FINAL THOUGHT FROM ZUBY

You only get ONE body and it has to last your entire life! So it's important to take care of it. If you build good eating and exercise habits early on, it will be easier for you to maintain them in the future. A healthy body also leads to a healthy mind, so be smart and take care of both!

www.TeamZuby.com
@Zubymusic

Join Asher as he celebrates

# Freedom Day

In Saga Two: Book 4

SAGA ONE BOX SET
GET THE COMPLETE SAGA ONE TODAY!
BRAVEBOOKS.COM